Keats, Ezra Jack.

Regards to the man in the moon.

$13.85

DATE			

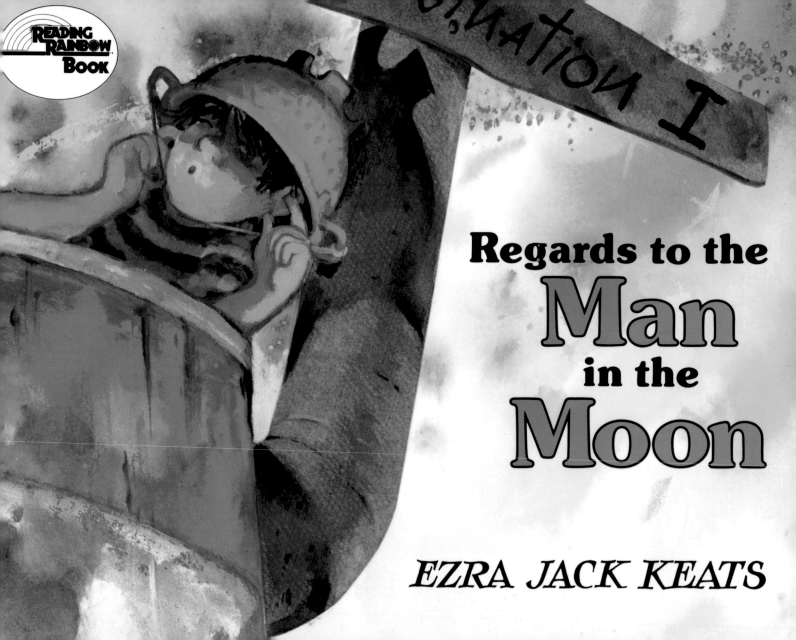

To the Glasers — Harold, Pearl, and David

Aladdin Paperbacks
An imprint of Simon & Schuster
Children's Publishing Division
1230 Avenue of the Americas
New York, NY 10020
Text copyright © 1981 by Ezra Jack Keats
All rights reserved including the right of reproduction
in whole or in part in any form.
First Aladdin Paperbacks edition

Printed in Hong Kong

15 14 13

Library of Congress Cataloging-in-Publication Data

Keats, Ezra Jack.
   Regards to the man in the moon.

   Summary: With help of his imagination, his
parents, and a few scraps of junk, Louie and his friends
travel through space.
   [1. Imagination—Fiction.   2. Play—Fiction]
I. Title.
PZ7.K2253Re   1986   [E]   86-28774
ISBN 0-689-71160-3 (pbk.)

Regards to the Man in the Moon

EZRA JACK KEATS

Aladdin Paperbacks

"What's up, Louie? Why so sad?"
Barney asked.
"The kids are laughin' at me."
"Laughin' at you! Why?"
"Well—"
"Come on, you c'n tell me.
I'm your Pop now."

"Well," Louie said, "they call you the junkman."
"Junk?" Barney growled. "They should know better than to call this junk. All a person needs is some imagination! And a little of that stuff can take you right out of this world. Watta' ya' say, Louie? Wanna give it a try?"

Louie and his parents got to work.
"What's goin' on?" the kids asked.
"I'm goin' outta this world,"
   Louie answered.

The kids snickered and nudged each other.
"Is that Voyager III?" they laughed.
"No," he said, "It's IMAGINATION I!"

"Well, don't run out of gas!"

"Regards to the Man in the Moon," they kidded.

"Are you going out there all alone?" Susie asked.

"Can I come with you, Louie? Can I?"

"Well, that depends—got lots of imagination?" he asked.

"Oh, yes," she said. "And—and I'll bring cookies, too!"
"Hmm, okay! Be here early tomorrow."

The next morning they climbed aboard. "Ready when you are," Susie shouted.

"Okay then," yelled Louie.
"Blast off!"
They held their breath.

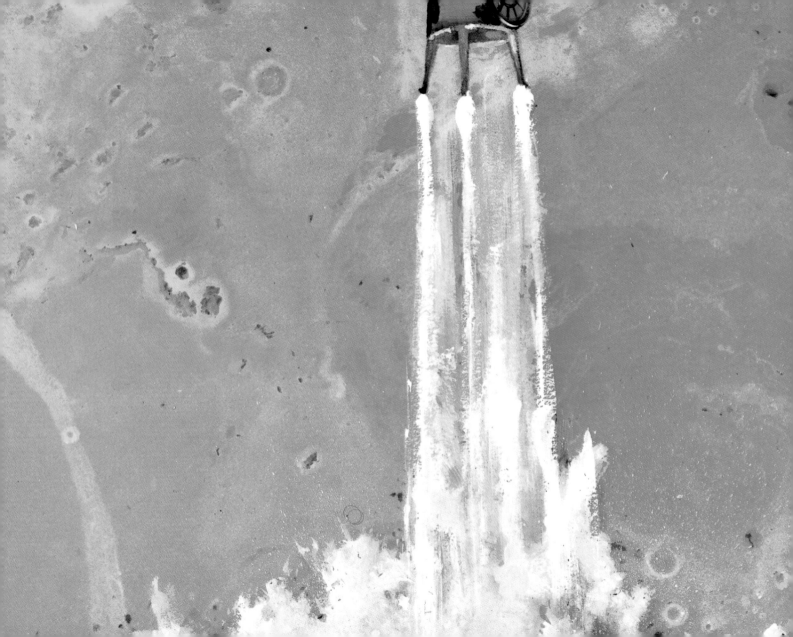

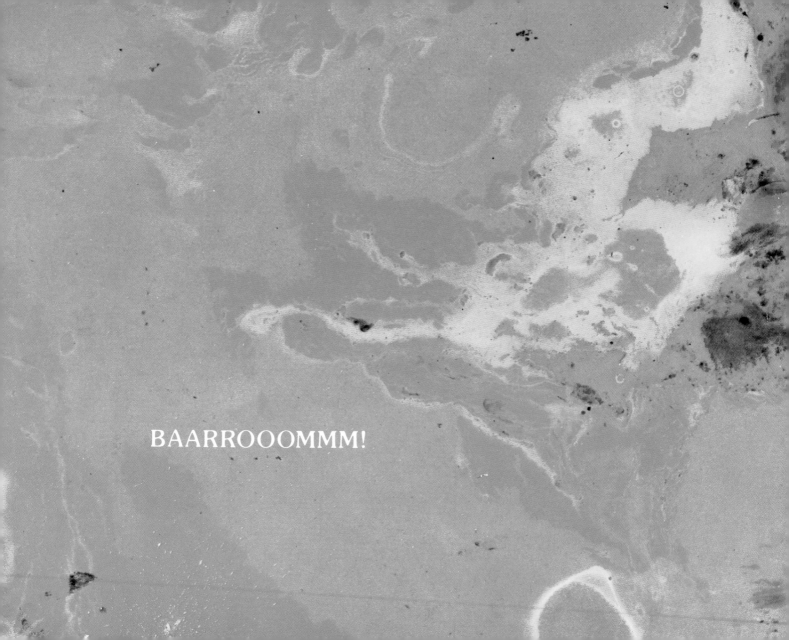

Way out in space they opened their eyes.

"We did it!" Susie gasped. They stared down at planet Earth.

"Everybody we know is down there—and we're all alone up here. I'm scared!"

"Me too!" Louie whispered.

They floated past strange and wondrous things...

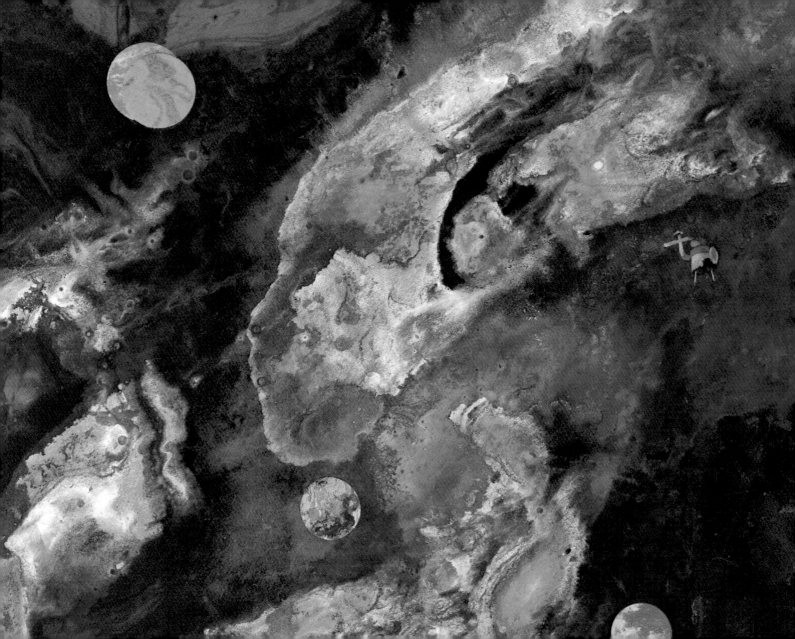

...and on through worlds no one had ever seen before.

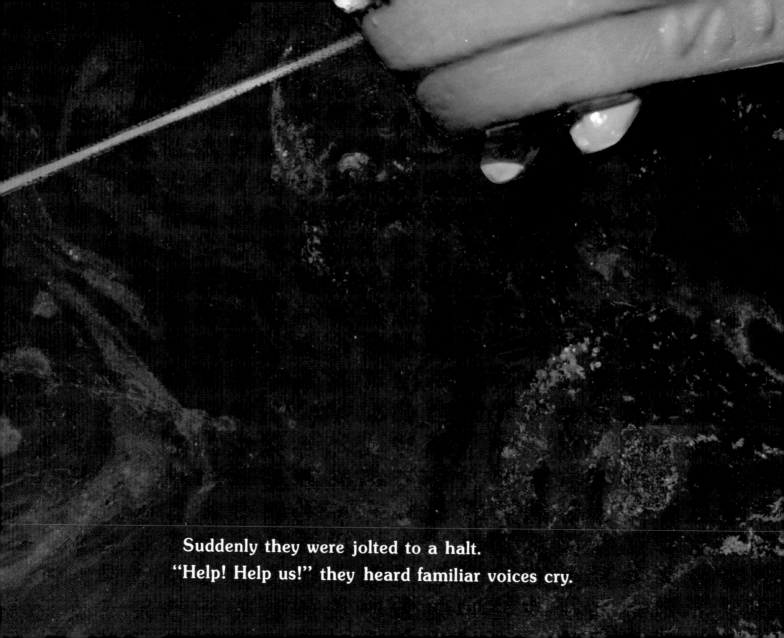

Suddenly they were jolted to a halt.
"Help! Help us!" they heard familiar voices cry.

It was Ziggie and Ruthie.
"We decided to follow you," Ziggie cried.
"But we've used up all our imagination.
We're stuck. We can't move. Don't untie us,
please, or we'll never get home."

"Let go!" Susie yelled.
"Or we'll all be stuck out here forever.
  You can only move on your own imagination!"
"Let go, will ya'," Louie cried. "There's a rock storm
  heading this way. We'll be smashed to bits!"

"They're not rocks! Can't you see?
  They're monsters!" Ziggie moaned.
"They're coming to capture us.
  We'll never see home again!"
"Monsters!" Susie said.
"Now you're using your imagination."
  They began to move.
"You're doin' fine now," Susie called, "so let go!
  You'll do better on your own and so will we."
  But Ziggie and Ruthie were so scared
  they just hung on.

and over—
and under—

They ducked this way—
and that—

and upside
down.

Finally the storm passed and they headed for home.

"Wow!" Ziggie joked nervously. "Wasn't that fun?"

"Yeah! We sure scared those monsters!" Ruthie bragged.

"Wish we could do it again!"

"And they thought," Louie said,

"they used up their imagination!"

They were getting close to home when Ziggie finally dropped the rope.

Next day they told everybody
about their adventures.
Soon all the kids were ready to take off.

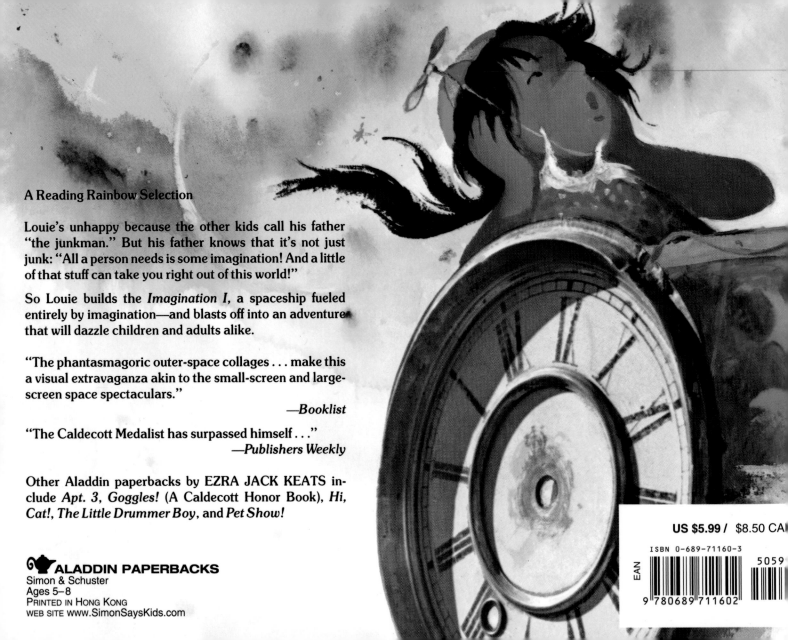

A Reading Rainbow Selection

Louie's unhappy because the other kids call his father "the junkman." But his father knows that it's not just junk: "All a person needs is some imagination! And a little of that stuff can take you right out of this world!"

So Louie builds the *Imagination I,* a spaceship fueled entirely by imagination—and blasts off into an adventure that will dazzle children and adults alike.

"The phantasmagoric outer-space collages . . . make this a visual extravaganza akin to the small-screen and large-screen space spectaculars."

—*Booklist*

"The Caldecott Medalist has surpassed himself . . ."
—*Publishers Weekly*

Other Aladdin paperbacks by EZRA JACK KEATS include *Apt. 3, Goggles!* (A Caldecott Honor Book), *Hi, Cat!, The Little Drummer Boy,* and *Pet Show!*

🫖 **ALADDIN PAPERBACKS**
Simon & Schuster
Ages 5–8
PRINTED IN HONG KONG
WEB SITE www.SimonSaysKids.com

US $5.99 / $8.50 CAN

ISBN 0-689-71160-3

EAN

5059

9 780689 711602